A Bright House

by
Alix Schwartz
& Matt Geiler

Story by **Alix Schwartz & Matt Geiler**
Written and Illustrated by **Matt Geiler**

Keep smiling 😊
it's contagious!
Alix Schwartz

PEACE and
MUCH LOVE,
Matt Geiler

BRIGHT
BOOKS
Los Angeles, California

B R I G H T
B O O K S

For information regarding permission, please write to:
Permissions Department
Bright Books/Positive Changemaker, LLC
25944 Coleridge Place
Stevenson Ranch, CA 91381

Bright Books and associated logos are trademarks
and/or registered trademarks of Positive Changemaker, LLC.

Book design by Matt Geiler · The text for this book is set in Goudy Bookletter 1911
The illustrations for this book are rendered in ink and colored digitally.

ISBN-13: 978-0-692-10874-1
1 2 3 4 5 6 7 8 9 10
Printed in the United States
First printing, July 2018

Alix For Robert and Annie, who believe in my dreams.
And for Michelle, who gave me hope.

Matt For Jenny, Edison, and Eliot, my brightest lights.

In a
sad
little house
near an
upside
down
town . . .

was a sad little boy with the saddest of frowns.

Around
Upside Down
Town
things were usually bad,

which is why this small boy was usually sad.

So she smiled at him.

And something peculiar and lovely took place ~

a bright spot appeared on his sad little face.

"What is THAT?" asked the boy as the spot gleamed through the gloom.

"That's what a smile does," chuckled Hope. "It fills up a room."

"Try it!" she said.
And so the boy did
and his bright spot balloooned
and became
SIX times
as big!

"I've never felt so **warm** and **shiny** before."

"You're **glowing!**" beamed Hope. "Let's do this some

Then Hope and the boy both **smiled hard** and the **light** in the **house** spilled out into the yard.

"Here's a good friend with stripes of maroon. He'll help you to float. It's a friendly balloon."

"This **encouraging** alarm clock **sings** you awake.

Here's a positive pencil

and an inspiring cupcake."

"Best of all, here's a
sturdy **stool**
to help when you try
to **touch** all those
hard to **reach**
places up
high."

The boy looked at all his new friends on the floor and knew that he wouldn't be lonely anymore.

"Thank you, Hope," he said, "for making me smile, for bringing these friends and staying awhile."

"Of course," Hope replied. "That's what smiles are about. You were always this bright. I just helped it come out."

Suddenly, the boy
realized the **reason** Hope came.

The sad little boy had a splendid new name.

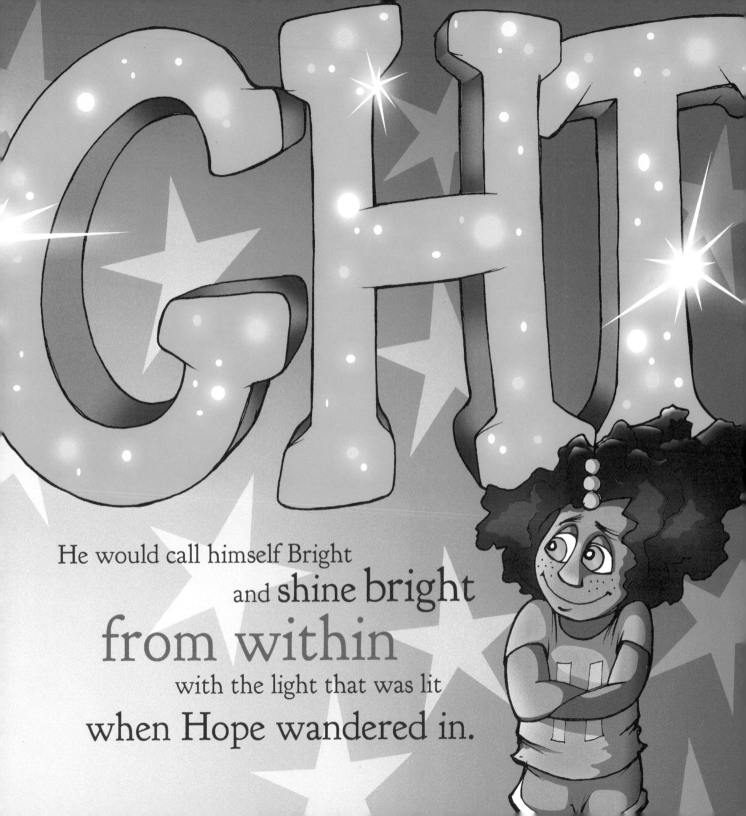

He would call himself Bright
and shine bright
from within
with the light that was lit
when Hope wandered in.

And all over
Upside Down Town
he would
let his
light out.

Bright and Hope will return in

Bright & Hope's
Wildest Dream

Join the adventure at
www.brightandhope.com

#adventuresofbrightandhope

CPSIA information can be obtained
at www.ICGtesting.com
Printed in the USA
BVHW02n0342090718
521122BV00002B/8/P

* 9 7 8 0 6 9 2 1 0 8 7 4 1 *